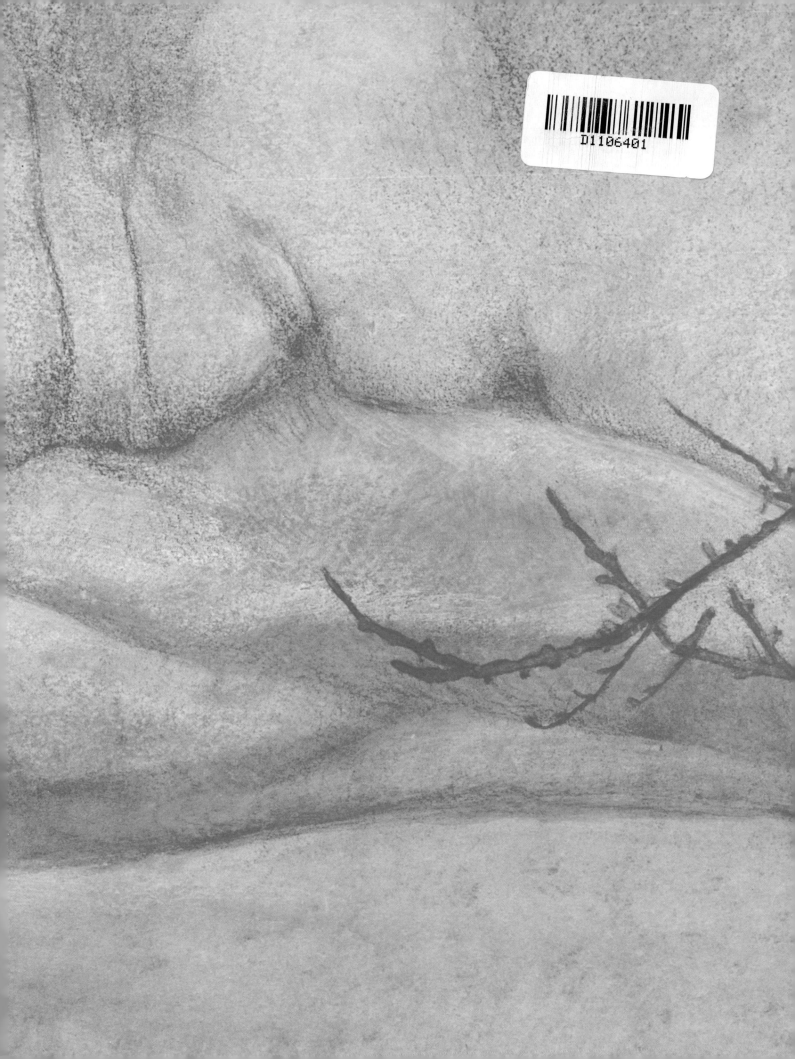

Islands

For Aileen, and for my mother, Margaret, whose lyrical
voice held us all spellbound for many a tale—A S

For Gérard Buèche—L G

Text copyright © 1995 by Anne Smythe
Illustrations copyright © 1995 by Laszlo Gal
First published in the United States in 1996
All rights reserved. No part of this book may be reproduced, stored
in a retrieval system or transmitted in any form or by any means,
without the prior written permission of the publisher, or in the case
of photocopying or other reprographic copying, a licence from
CANCOPY (Canadian Reprography Collective), Toronto, Ontario.

Groundwood Books/Douglas & McIntyre
585 Bloor Street West
Toronto, Ontario M6G 1K5

The publisher gratefully acknowledges the assistance of the Canada
Council, the Ontario Arts Council and the Ontario Ministry of
Culture, Tourism and Recreation.

Canadian Cataloguing in Publication Data

Smythe, Anne, 1951-
Islands
ISBN 0-88899-238-6

I. Gal, Laszlo. II. Title.

PS8587.M9717 1995   jC813'.54   C95-931521-7
PZ7.S58Is 1995

The illustrations are done in oil on board
Design by Michael Solomon
Printed and bound in Hong Kong by Everbest Printing Co. Ltd.

Islands

Anne Smythe

ILLUSTRATED BY

Laszlo Gal

A GROUNDWOOD BOOK

Douglas & McIntyre Vancouver / Toronto

Laura, dressed in her shiny purple parka, laced up her bright new skates. Perched on the rock where she always sat to catch minnows, she now saw that the warm water, which had tickled her feet in the hot summer sun, was frozen solid and clear as crystal. She could hardly believe this was the same place she'd been swimming only a few months before. Ribbons of snow shifted this way and that as she stared across to the islands in the distance.

I am going to skate to those islands, all the way to Swimming Rock, thought Laura, and she pulled her laces as tightly as she could, tied a double bow at the top of her skates, and stood up.

Swimming Rock was on the farthest of three islands that stood in the middle of this not-so-large oval lake. Laura remembered how the water had rippled and glittered as she'd paddled toward those islands with her father in the green canoe this past summer. It had seemed a long way away.

Laura pulled her soft new scarf up around her nose and skated in circles while she waited for her mom. Finally her mother stood attaching a round red flying saucer to the belt of her backpack.

Laura set off, her skates skirring over the ice. The sun shone like a soft, hazy globe above the trees on the far shore.

As she slid over thin cracks in the ice surface, she whispered, "Step on a crack, you break your mother's..."

Oh, oh, she thought, that one did crack.

Laura stopped and turned, waiting for her mom to catch up. *Snap!* There it went again.

"Mom?" she called, as her mother skated up beside her. "Is the ice thick enough?"

"Twenty inches thick yesterday," said her mother.

"How many centimeters is that?" asked Laura.

Her mom laughed and put her hands up to show her just how thick the ice was.

"That's thicker than a twenty-layer birthday cake," said Laura and, taking a deep breath, she set out again.

Laura watched for bumps, but the ice was as smooth as could be. The only marks were those of other skaters who'd been there before her. These made long thin curvy lines like spider webs cut deep into the blue-gray ice. As Laura listened to the sound her own skates made, she wondered what the fish might be hearing way down below. She could imagine them scared and scurrying away to another part of the lake, huddling together in the dark depths.

My feet are getting cold, she thought, but I'm not stopping now.

Laura and her mother were more than halfway to the first island. Clouds covered the sun. The air had become still and heavy. She kept going. The islands were her favorite place in the whole world. Sometimes sitting at her desk at school in the city, she could almost smell the pine trees. And even now, as she thought of that pungent scent in the soft summer breeze, her feet felt a little warmer.

Craaack, craaack, vroooom.

Laura turned and there, rumbling across the lake toward her, was a large blue pickup truck.

"Don't worry," said her mother as she skated closer. "This truck was out here yesterday, too. The people who live here know about ice. They only drive out onto it when it's safe."

Laura stood staring as the truck approached. It turned and stopped, not too far from the first island.

A boy and a man jumped out. They walked over to a bump on the ice, bent down and stared.

"That's Henderson's truck," said Laura's mom.

"Can we go see what they're doing?" asked Laura.

"Sure," said her mom, and they skated over to where the boy was now swinging a pickax onto the ice. Laura could see he was chipping away at a hole that was partly frozen over. She knew what he was doing. She skated a little closer, but not too close.

"What are you catching?" she asked.

"Splake," he announced. He swung the pick down hard and shards of ice flew up.

"What's splake?"

"Oh," said the boy, "it's a kind of trout. This is the only time of year they'll bite. They live too far down in the summer and besides, there's lots to eat then."

"Oh," said Laura.

By now the boy had opened the hole. Water splurted out. He took his pole and, sitting on a wooden crate, he lowered it into the fishing hole. Laura peered a little closer. She was longing to see a fish swim by.

Just then, ever so quietly, sprinkles of snow began to fall.

"Well, good luck with the splake," said Laura. "I've got to go."

Laura glided off through the feathery flakes of silently tumbling snow to the first island. The island was so small and rocky that the only creatures Laura had ever seen there were the turtles who sunned themselves by the dozen on its shore in the summer.

"No sign of them now," she murmured.

Dug into the mud somewhere, she thought, and in her mind's eye she could see them wrapped in the bank of the lake, fast asleep.

She skated on toward the tall pines of the second island. The large, slow-falling flakes fluttered against the green of the pine boughs.

Laura noticed that her feet had a strange, aching, tingling feeling. She decided to change into her boots. Her feet would be a little warmer, and she'd be able to explore better.

She dragged herself up the rocks at the edge of the middle island. Snow lay in amongst the trees as she pulled off her skates in a quiet, cocoon-like space among the pines.

"Animal tracks," she whispered. "I wonder whose they are?"

She shimmied across the floor of the tiny sheltered wood, careful not to smudge the trail of markings.

"Mom!" she shouted. "Come see!"

"They're deer tracks," she whispered as her mother finally ducked beneath the trees.

"Yes. Yes, they are," said Laura's mom.

Laura knew they were deer tracks, because she had an old book with sketches of the different kinds of markings you could find in the woods.

"These are the tracks of a female deer," said her mother. "You can tell by the size and this cleft here."

Laura peered closer.

"And smaller ones, female, too—a mother and her fawn, just like us out here on the island. Looking for food, I bet," she said.

Then she remembered the snack her mother had packed for them.

"Mom," she asked, "could we leave them an apple, just in case they come back?"

"Well," said her mother, "we only have two, but sure, we'll give them mine."

"No," said Laura firmly. "We'll leave them one and share the other."

Smiling, Laura handed her mother a plump round Ida Red apple. Laura hollowed out a small nest of scattered pine boughs, twigs and snow on the ground beneath the tall trees. Then she nestled the apple in the middle.

"There," she said. "They'll have a nice treat waiting for them when they come back the next time." Then her mother took her penknife and cut their apple in two, and Laura remembered the time they'd sat in this very spot, the summer the storm had sprung out of nowhere and forced them off the lake. There was no sign of a storm now. Just the quietly falling snow and the *chickadee-dee-dee* overhead.

Snow was falling faster as they plodded the last few steps to the third island. Laura walked right over to Swimming Rock and stood beneath it as it jutted out over the lake. She looked up and remembered how she had jumped way up into the air and splashed into the water that was now the ice under her feet.

"Come on, Laura," said her mom. "Here's a place to climb."

Laura clambered up the cleft in the side of the rock and peered down. Yikes! It falls off pretty suddenly, she thought. But then she saw a place where the drop was not quite so steep.

This was a perfect slide, the kind that otters would love, she thought. She positioned her saucer carefully, slipping it into place and taking a deep breath. "One, two, three..." She was off.

Shooooo.

"What if I go through?" called Laura. *Bang!* "Eeeeee..."

She crashed onto the hard surface and the saucer went whirring and spinning like a top, way out onto the ice. Laura laughed and scrambled back to the shore to climb the steep rock again. And again and again. Even her mother took a turn, and she hollered, too, as the saucer crunched down hard onto the ice.

Finally, when Laura was quite exhausted, she and her mom sat down to drink their hot chocolate. Two chick-adees chattered to each other above their heads as they drank the steamy warm chocolate milk that Laura's mom poured from a silvery thermos. Snowflakes fell into Laura's cup and melted very quickly, as she drank up every drop. The taste of hot chocolate reminded her of the freshly baked bread and her grandmother's raspberry jam waiting on the kitchen table.

Though there was quite a thick blanket of snow cover-ing the ice by now, Laura insisted on skating back. It wasn't easy to pull those cold skates back on her feet, but she did.

It felt strange to skate when she could no longer see the ice. Snow collected on her skates as she went, so she glided along a little more cautiously this time.

Still, it wasn't long before she was sailing past Henderson's truck.

"Any luck?" she called to the Henderson boy, who was standing by the fishing hole. With a proud grin, he held up a string of five good-sized splake.

Laura smiled, waved and kept skating.

When she finally came in sight of her own shore, Laura stopped to look back at the islands one last time.

As quietly as it had begun, the snow stopped and the sun burst forth, dazzling a bright sparkling whiteness. This gave Laura an idea. She lay on her back and started to wave her arms up and down and move her legs back and forth on the ice. She made a second, then a third sparkling angel in the fresh, glittering snow.

She stood and beamed down at her creations, wings touching wings in a circular pattern, dusted with tiny jewel-like crystals, all colors of the rainbow.

"Now," said Laura, standing tall, "I'm going to make a wish."

A blue jay shrieked from the shore, and she thought again of the warm kitchen that was waiting for her, so she winked at her snow angels, then turned back toward the rock where her journey had begun.

That night, when Laura was tucked snugly into bed, her stomach full of fresh-baked bread, she said to her mother, "If you promise you won't say anything, I'll tell you the wish I made out on the lake today."

"Promise," said her mother.

"Well," Laura whispered, "I wished that the snow angels would come alive and dance out there tonight."

"Oh," said her mother softly. "Well, if you close your eyes and listen, you might hear something."

So Laura closed her eyes and, sure enough, she began to hear from outside her window a high, soft, tinkling sound. She took a deep breath and found herself drifting into a warm and feathery sleep, where she saw a mother deer and her yearling, their noses sniffing a certain bright red apple that was nestled under the pine boughs of Laura's favorite place in all the world.

And out there, on the snow-covered lake, she saw three
swirling figures dancing in the soft, silvery light of the moon.